MARK BILLINGHAM

CUT OFF

sphere

SPHERE

First published in Great Britain in 2017 by Sphere

1 3 5 7 9 10 8 6 4 2

A CIP catalogue record for this book
is available from the British Library.

ISBN 978-0-7515-6889-9

Typeset in Stone Serif by M Rules
Printed and bound in Great Britain by
Clays Ltd, St Ives plc

Papers used by Sphere are from well-managed forests
and other responsible sources.

Sphere
An imprint of
Little, Brown Book Group
Carmelite House
50 Victoria Embankment
London EC4Y 0DZ

An Hachette UK Company
www.hachette.co.uk

www.littlebrown.co.uk

Chapter One

Louise

Mid-morning on a Saturday, and as usual, the café was packed.

It was a small, noisy room at the rear of a vintage home-ware shop. Second-hand furniture and bric-a-brac in the front of the place, coffee and homemade cake being served at the back. A smiley young waitress with a nose-ring moved between the smaller tables. Louise, Stephen and Andrew sat at the long table that ran the length of one wall. It was all a bit squashed, because they were sharing it with several others.

'Come on then, Steven Spielberg,' Andrew said. 'Let's see.'

Louise opened the camera app on her phone and handed it across. Stephen squeezed closer to

1

Andrew so that the pair of them could watch the video Louise had shot that morning.

'I'm pretty pleased with it, actually,' Louise said.

'I'll be looking out for the Oscar,' Stephen said.

Andrew pressed PLAY.

It was a series of scenes and images from around the town.

A young man with a heavy beard playing guitar opposite Boots while shoppers queue outside a posh bakery.

An elderly couple standing in the doorway of an old-fashioned ice-cream parlour.

Tea-coloured sea lashing against the shingle.

A stuffed seagull sitting next to a display of cushions in a shop window.

Morris dancers performing for a small crowd in front of a pub. They're wearing bells, waving hankies and clattering sticks ...

The video finished.

Louise reached across the table to click out of the camera app, and took her phone back. She quickly checked to see if any emails had arrived.

None had.

'What do you think?'

Andrew nodded. 'Very nice,' he said.

Stephen shuddered. 'I think Morris dancers are spooky.'

'Yeah, me too, but that's why I do all these films down here. This place is full of . . . oddballs, and the editor loves all that weird stuff.' Louise had been hired by a fashion magazine to find locations for photo shoots. 'Weirder the better.' She put her phone down and picked up her coffee. 'Skinny models prancing around with freaks in the background.' She laughed, then looked at Andrew and Stephen. 'You do like it, though? You think it's good?'

'We'll have another look when we get home,' Andrew said. 'Have you put it online yet?'

Louise nodded. 'Yeah. It's in the public file on PhotoBox, same as usual.'

Andrew stroked the small dog on his lap. 'You going to be around for the shoot?'

'Yeah, if they like these locations.'

'Of course they will,' Andrew said.

'Hope so. I don't get paid otherwise.'

'I'll organise dinner then. You bringing Danny?' Andrew winked at Stephen.

Louise rolled her eyes and picked up her phone again. 'If I didn't know any better, I might think you preferred my boyfriend to me.'

Andrew pretended to be shocked. 'How *could* you?'

'I'm right, aren't I?'

'Well, you're more fun to hang out with,'

Stephen said. He leaned back and slid an arm around his boyfriend's shoulder. 'But Danny's definitely got better legs.'

Andrew nodded. 'Definitely,' he said.

'I'll have to settle for that then,' Louise said. Checking her phone again, she glanced at the people sharing their table. Next to Andrew, an old man read a newspaper, folding it noisily. The woman sitting close to Louise had her head bent over her own phone. Louise could just about hear the beeps and tweets of her game over the chatter of the other customers. The woman shook her head and muttered to herself as she stabbed at the screen. She turned away every minute or so to drop a small piece of rock cake on to the floor. It was quickly gobbled up by the scruffy black dog lying between her chair and Louise's.

'Good boy,' the woman said.

The dog looked up at her, hungry for more.

Behind the small counter the coffee machine hissed angrily.

Stephen drank the last of his mint tea. 'Seriously though, it would be so nice if you could get down here a bit more.' He pulled his own phone across and began scrolling. 'We only get to see you one weekend in three or whatever.'

Louise stopped tapping at the screen of her handset. She reached across to pat Stephen's hand. 'I want to, but work's a bit full-on at the moment. Same for Danny.'

'Shame,' Stephen said.

'Anyway, I thought you hated us Down-From-London types.'

'Only the boring ones,' Stephen said, still scrolling through his phone.

'Right, that's it.' Andrew leaned forward suddenly and snatched the phones from Louise and Stephen. They stared at him.

'What the hell are you doing?' Stephen asked.

Smiling, Andrew laid the two phones down next to his own. He lined them up carefully. 'There.'

'There, what?' Louise looked at Stephen and shook her head. She was every bit as confused as he was.

'First one to pick up their phone pays for the drinks.' Andrew grinned and looked at them both. 'First one to even *look* at their phone ...'

'What?' Stephen glared at his partner.

'Look at us,' Andrew said. 'Honestly, it's mad how ... addicted we all are to them. Texting, emailing, whatever. Like bloody junkies. I mean, whatever happened to the fine art of conversation?'

'Don't be stupid.' Stephen moved a hand towards his phone, but Andrew slapped it away.

'Starting now,' Andrew said. 'I bet none of us can make five minutes.'

'Seriously?' Stephen widened his eyes. 'Five minutes?'

'You're on,' Louise said.

Stephen sighed and folded his arms. Louise and Andrew sat back and for half a minute they stared at one another. The three of them listened to the conversations of people around them. They studied the old posters and signs that lined the walls. Stephen removed his glasses and began to clean them, while Louise reached down to stroke the scruffy black dog near her feet. Andrew smiled at the waitress when she came over to the table. He whispered a 'Thank you' as she gathered up the empty plates and cups. The girl smiled back, but she looked puzzled.

Why were these three so quiet suddenly? They had not stopped chattering since they came in.

'Everything OK?' the waitress asked.

'Fine,' Louise said.

'Can I get you anything else?'

'Oh, fuck this . . . '

The waitress watched as Andrew sat forward, grabbed his phone and immediately began typing in his PIN. Stephen and Louise laughed and high-fived. They were enjoying their moment of triumph as they reached for their own phones.

'I think you lose,' Louise said.

Andrew stuck his tongue out at her.

Stephen was still laughing. 'So who's the biggest phone junkie, then?'

Andrew shrugged and pulled a twenty-pound note from his wallet. 'It's only a couple of coffees, for Christ's sake . . .'

Chapter Two

Louise

Ten minutes later the three of them were walking slowly around the busy market in the small car park behind the church. It was part of their regular Saturday morning routine whenever Louise was in town. Coffee, gossip, then the market. The first few rows of the market were taken up with fresh fruit and vegetables, flowers and fast food. Elsewhere there were stalls selling used tools, CDs and vinyl. Others sold vintage china and bits of furniture that had been made to look older than they really were.

Tinny-sounding jazz drifted from speakers mounted on a van. Louise tried to persuade a grumpy stall-holder to take fifteen pounds for a set of metal spice jars. While Stephen and

8

Andrew checked out a ratty-looking stuffed owl. Their little dog was yapping at their feet.

It was dry, but the wind blowing in off the channel was as fierce as usual.

Louise left the stall-holder to his over-priced knick-knacks and wandered towards a stall selling bread, cheese and the like. The prices were as mad as always. Two tubs of olives would have cost almost as much as those bloody spice jars. As she tried to decide between chilli and garlic, she reached into her pocket for her phone.

She was horrified to see that the phone in her hand was not her phone.

She said, 'What the . . . ?'

She stared at the screen for a few seconds, then turned to hurry across to Stephen and Andrew.

'Did either of you pick up my phone?'

Stephen looked at her.

'Have you got my *phone*?'

Andrew put down a stuffed red squirrel, which was even tattier than the owl, and dug his phone from his pocket. He shook his head. 'Sorry, darling.'

'Nope.' Stephen held his Blackberry towards her. Its brightly coloured case was easy to see.

'Look at this.' Louise handed Andrew the iPhone she had picked up from the table in the café. The cover was greasy and the screen was cracked. He stared at it and pulled a face.

'It's definitely not yours.'

'I know,' Louise said. She was starting to sweat a little.

'Oh dear,' Andrew said. 'Well, don't panic.'

'That's easy for you to say.'

Stephen was already dialling Louise's number. 'It's ringing . . .'

They waited.

'How did you manage to do that?' Andrew asked, handing back the mystery phone.

'No idea. I must just have picked up the wrong one.'

Stephen shook his head. 'It's gone straight to Answerphone.'

'Shit . . .'

Louise turned and pushed her way back through the crowd. Dodging cars, she sprinted across the road and was out of breath by the time she got back to the café. She looked frantically around. She could see that their seats had already been taken. But she recognised the old man, who was still there reading his newspaper.

She leaned down, holding out the phone that wasn't hers. 'Excuse me, but is this yours?'

The old man said nothing.

'Did you pick up the wrong phone, by any chance?'

The old man lowered his paper. 'Sorry, what did you say?'

'Have you got my phone?'

The old man smiled and lifted his paper again. 'I haven't got a phone, love.'

Louise turned away and stepped quickly across to the counter. The young girl with the nose-ring looked up, but was busy serving another customer. Louise leaned across anyway.

'I don't suppose you know who that woman was? The one who was sitting next to me?' Louise pointed back at the long table. 'I think she's taken my phone by mistake.'

'Sorry, who?'

The customer was giving Louise a very dirty look, but Louise ignored him.

'The woman who was sitting *there*.' She pointed again. 'Ten minutes ago.'

The waitress handed a plate of cake to her customer. He walked away, muttering. Something about rudeness.

'What did she look like?' the girl asked.

Louise tried to remember, but she had barely taken the woman in. 'I'm not really sure.'

'Old? Young?'

'She had a dog,' Louise said.

The girl nodded at someone in the corner who was waving and asking for their bill. She looked back to Louise. 'Sorry, I've only just started working here. I don't know everyone yet.'

'A black dog?'

'Have you tried calling it?'

'Sorry?' For a moment, Louise had thought the waitress was talking about calling the dog.

The girl began putting teacups on to a tray. 'Have you tried calling your phone.'

'Yes, obviously.' Louise swallowed a curse and looked down at the strange phone. It was locked and asking for a PIN number. She tried 1-2-3-4, then all but slammed it on to the counter in frustration.

'I'd go mental if I lost mine,' the girl said.

Louise just nodded. The panic was starting to build. Sweat was running down her collar, tickling her shoulder blade.

'She'll probably call you as soon as she realises.' The girl smiled. 'You know, she'll call the numbers in your address book or whatever.'

Louise was barely listening. She was thinking about everything that was on her missing phone. All those important emails and texts. Her contacts' phone numbers and email addresses. Some of that stuff would be on her computer, but she was useless at backing things up. She hadn't had a chance to transfer the film from this morning . . .

The girl came from behind the counter to deliver the bill to the small table in the corner. When she came back, she leaned on the counter and said, 'Why don't you leave your name?'

'What?'

'Leave your name and address, then I can let you know if she brings it back. I mean, I'm sure she will.' The waitress wiped her hands, opened a drawer and pulled out a piece of paper.

Louise sighed and took it. She began searching in her bag for a pen.

'She wouldn't have taken it on purpose.'

Louise grunted, scribbling her name.

'Nobody round here would do anything like that.'

Louise handed the piece of paper back. She turned to look at the other customers, just in case. She leaned down to peer beneath the tables.

There were only crumbs and dust.

'It's not that kind of place,' the waitress said.

Chapter Three

Louise

Louise slammed her front door and walked through to the kitchen. She peeled off her running top and took a bottle of water from the fridge, easing the phone from her bum-bag as she swigged. She'd run without headphones for fear of not hearing it ring. She'd heard nothing, but she wanted to make sure.

There were no missed calls. No text messages.

Over an hour now, and still the woman hadn't tried to get in touch.

Jogging along the edge of the beach, she'd thought about nothing else. Normally a nice long run was a good way to clear her head. It was usually when she came up with all her best ideas, but not today. The wind had picked up and it had started to drizzle, but all she could think about was how important her phone was. The things on it that she needed. Her music and her voice messages. The pictures of her mum and dad, her brother and his kids, her and the girls on the holiday to Crete.

Stuff for work, private stuff ... *lots* of stuff.

Her whole life was on that phone, for God's sake.

She guzzled the last of the water and tossed the plastic bottle into the recycling bin. She stood, breathing heavily for a minute or so, staring at the phone. Then she picked it up and trudged upstairs.

Who doesn't look at their phone for an hour?

Maybe it *was* still in the café somewhere. She wondered if she should go back and take another look. Maybe the waitress had taken it. Maybe she was only pretending to be helpful, and it was in the little bitch's pocket the whole bloody time.

After all, you couldn't really trust anyone, could you?

In the bedroom, she stripped off the rest of her sticky clothes. She stared at herself in the full-length mirror. Naked with the phone in her hand. She carried it through to the en-suite bathroom and placed it on a small shelf above the sink, where she usually put her own phone. She watched it for a minute or so until she began to feel cold, then stepped into the shower and stared at it through the glass.

She'd bought the house – three bedrooms, two bathrooms, a stone's throw from the beach – just over a year ago. A second home by the sea. A bolt-hole. It was actually bigger than her place in London and she'd been amazed at how cheap it was. Well, compared to prices in London, anyway.

A month or so after buying it, she'd got together with Danny and, for a while, the two of them had made the drive down every weekend. Lately though, he had seemed rather less keen on making the trip. It was fine with her, because she knew how busy his job kept him. They were *both* busy, and the truth was that she didn't really mind being here on her own. She was able to relax and pamper herself a bit. Curling up in front of some trashy TV and listening to the sea.

Recently she had been finding it harder to get away herself, but there was plenty of fun to be had when she was here. She'd clicked with Stephen and Andrew right away, and they had introduced her to plenty of locals. The local 'weirdos', Danny called them. She'd met plenty of others who came down from London too. The DFLs. They always seemed keen to go out for a meal, or while away the afternoon in one coffee shop or another.

There was nothing not to like.

'You should move down here,' Stephen was fond of telling her.

'You could always commute,' Andrew had said.

'Seriously?'

'Why not?'

'It's an hour and a half each way! And that's if the trains are running.'

'Don't you prefer it here?' Andrew had asked.

'It's a mad idea ...'

Now and then, on a Northern Line train, tight against some sweaty bastard in rush hour, Louise had given it serious thought.

She had loved the house from the moment she had set foot in it. She had felt at home here instantly. The town was quirky and the people were friendlier than she was used to. Or maybe it was just because she'd grown up by the sea and missed the smell and the noise of it.

Whatever the reason, within minutes of unloading the car on a Friday night and turning the heating on, she would usually feel herself starting to unwind a little. She would mooch around or ride her bike. She would listen to music and read magazines. It was easy enough to deal with any messages and emails when they arrived, and by Saturday lunchtime she would be dreading the Sunday afternoon drive back to London.

She looked forward to coming here so much.

Now though, she was tense and panicky. Her skin prickled and her heart raced. Stretched out on the sofa in a DKNY jogging suit, with a glass of wine to hand and Mumford & Sons on the stereo, Louise felt anything but relaxed.

She could not settle.

She flicked through the latest issue of the fashion magazine she was currently working with. But she was unable to focus. Every few minutes, her eyes would drift from the latest designer dress or posh handbag to the ever-silent handset on the cushion beside her.

Stupid, *stupid* thing.

She reached across and picked it up. She knew that some people had problems remembering PIN numbers, so she punched in 0-0-0-0 just in case.

The phone remained locked.

'Fuck!'

She tossed the phone back on to the sofa and opened the magazine again. She put it down a few moments later.

She looked at her watch. Three hours now. It was impossible to imagine anyone not looking at a phone for that long. What the hell was the woman doing?

She stood up, taking her wine glass with her and began slowly pacing the room. It felt smaller and uglier than usual and there seemed to be less ... air, somehow.

It felt as though she'd never been in the room before.

Chapter Four

Louise

'Why the hell doesn't she answer the phone?' Louise tried not to sound whiny, but couldn't help herself. She sounded like a teenager. Pissed off because she couldn't get what she wanted.

She could hear the voice of her dad.

Well, we can't always get what we want.

But for most of her life Louise had got exactly what she wanted. The job, the nice houses, the perfect boyfriend. She'd earned those things, though. She'd worked hard, and someone as attractive as her was never going to end up with an average boyfriend, were they? Some people did better than others. That was the way of the world. Hating not getting what she wanted didn't make her spoiled, did it?

'I mean, seriously.' Louise's jaw was aching.

She'd been grinding her teeth in frustration all day. 'Why isn't she answering my phone?'

'I'll keep trying,' Danny said. 'Have you tried Find my iPhone?'

'I never set it up.'

'Why not?'

'Because I'm useless, all right? This isn't helping, you know.'

'Sorry ...'

'Andrew and Stephen called her, *you've* been calling her. I'm sure I didn't leave it on silent.'

'I'll keep ringing.' Danny shrugged. 'She's got to answer eventually.'

'Yeah, I suppose.'

They were talking on Skype and, like most people did when they were making video calls, Louise was actually looking at the image of herself. Her face in the small square at the bottom of the computer screen. She thought she'd looked better. Now, she flicked her eyes to Danny. 'Thanks.'

'No worries.' Danny had several days' stubble. He looked as gorgeous as always, even in the black beanie hat he was rarely seen without. He was looking at himself, too. He was every bit as vain as she was. Probably more.

Louise leaned away from her laptop and picked up the phone from the desk. It was exactly the same size and shape as hers. The cases were similar too, but she still could not believe that she had mistaken it for her own. It was more than a bit grubby for a start, and it had a stupid lock-screen photo: that same scruffy dog Louise had seen underneath the table in the café that morning. She had simply reached for this phone without looking. She must have done.

God, how could she have been so careless?

'Piece of shit thing.' She dropped it on the table. 'You know, I don't even think it's a 6S.'

'So, how come you thought it was yours?'

'I *didn't* think it was mine.'

'Don't take it out on me,' Danny said. He sighed and slid a hand across his stubble.

'I don't know,' Louise said. 'I just grabbed it when we were leaving. Now she's sitting there with a brand new iPhone 6S and I've got ... *this*.'

She dropped the phone back on the desk, then jumped slightly as a seagull screamed just outside the back window. They were fearless and cheeky, like London pigeons. They were a nuisance too, shitting all over the front steps, and Louise had to admit that she was a little frightened of them.

The last time she'd been down for the weekend, she'd found a seagull sitting on top of her car. She'd just got back from her run and seen it perched there, like it owned the bloody place. Up close, it was huge and she could see that its beak was razor sharp. The horrible thing had just stared at her. She'd been close enough to see herself reflected in its beady black eye.

She'd turned away quickly before the bird could fly at her face. She'd run into the house.

'So, how did the filming go?' Danny was happily chugging on an e-cigarette the size of a walkie-talkie. It kept him off cigarettes, he said, but Louise knew very well that he still smoked when he was on his own. She could smell it on him. 'Get some good stuff?'

'Fine,' Louise said. 'It's all on my phone though, the footage I shot. I was showing it to Stephen and Andrew in the café.' She reached for her wine glass and took a sip. 'I'll probably have to do it all over again now. Buy another bloody phone.'

'You'll get it back.'

'She's probably sold it already.'

'You can claim it on insurance. Buy a nice, shiny new one.'

'I want the one I've got.' She was sounding like that stroppy teenager again, but she couldn't help herself.

'Look, I said . . . I'll keep trying and as soon as I get through I'll Skype you, OK?'

Louise took another sip of wine, stared at the stupid, *shitty* phone.

'Lou?'

'Yeah. Thanks.'

'So, how are Stephen and Andrew?' Danny asked.

'Don't worry, they still love you.'

'Who can blame them?'

Louise said, 'Maybe the battery's dead.'

'What battery?'

'On my phone.'

Danny shook his head, and spoke through a cloud of vapour. 'It's ringing, isn't it? If it was dead, it would go straight to voicemail.'

'I charged it up last night.'

'There you go then.'

Louise glanced at her watch. She said, 'Why don't you come down?'

'When?'

'You could get a train.'

'You want me to come down just because you've lost your bloody phone?'

'No.' Yes. Actually, right about now, she could do with some support. A little sympathy. But she wasn't going to tell Danny that. 'Because I want to see you.'

'You know I can't.'

'Why not?'

24

'Because I've got stuff to do.'

'What stuff?'

'Maybe next weekend.'

They said nothing for ten or fifteen seconds.

Louise had picked up the phone again. She was rubbing it against her leg, trying to clean the dirty, cracked screen. She thought about her own phone, clean and lovely in its expensive case, and remembered what Andrew had said in the café that morning. About them being like junkies. Now, she knew what he meant.

OK, so not having her phone wasn't quite like being desperate for crack or heroin. Not that she'd know what *that* was like. But she guessed it was the same sort of ... need. An itch that she couldn't scratch. The feeling that she was missing out on something important. The knowledge that having it back again would make everything feel so much better.

When she looked back at her laptop, Danny had turned away, distracted by something.

'Anyway, I'd like to see how calm *you'd* be.'

Danny looked back at her. He puffed on his e-cig and blew out a cloud of bluish smoke. 'What?'

'If you lost your phone. You'd be a basket case.'

'Yeah, probably,' Danny said.

'So, stop making out like I'm over-reacting.'

'Well, don't you think you *are*? Just a little bit.'

'It's annoying,' Louise said. 'That's all. I'm just annoyed.'

The truth was, it felt as if her right arm had been cut off. Every few minutes, there would be a moment of terrible agony. When she thought, *Oh, I must check such and such,* or *I need to look at* ... Then she would remember that she couldn't, and it was like a punch in the stomach.

Louise had been lucky. She had never lost anyone close to her. But she thought this must be what grief felt like.

On her laptop screen, Danny smiled. He said, 'Listen, I need to get on. I'll Skype you later, all right? What time are you going to bed?'

'It doesn't matter.'

'You have to go to bed at some point. You'll be exhausted.'

'I'll be fine,' Louise said.

'You look exhausted already.'

'Oh, thanks.'

'Exhausted, but still hot.'

That made Louise smile, and it felt good. She hadn't smiled since the moment she'd discovered her phone was gone. 'Look, however late it is, if you get through, I want to know.'

'Right.'

'Just keep trying my phone.'

'I *said* I would.' Danny leaned towards the screen. 'Now give us a kiss, mardy-arse.' He leaned closer still, his puckered lips filling the screen.

Chapter Five

Louise

The church near the castle rang the four o'clock bell. On TV, a snooty couple from Suffolk were being shown around a house they would not buy, while Louise dozed on the sofa. She had been asleep for half an hour, wrung out with frustration and having drunk half a bottle of wine.

She was dreaming about Danny. She was trying to reach him, but the smoke coming out of his mouth was too thick. She lost sight of him and started to cry. She was calling out his name, but he couldn't hear her. She thought she could hear him laughing, and somewhere far away, a phone was ringing ...

She was wide awake within seconds. She gasped and scrabbled for the handset.

'Thank Christ ...'

28

'Oh, hello.' There was silence for a few, crackly seconds. 'Sorry to bother you, but I think this is your phone.' The woman on the other end of the line sounded shy and unsure. Her voice was gentle. There was no accent Louise could recognise.

Louise was already on her feet and walking around. She grabbed the remote to turn the TV down. 'That's right.'

'The one I'm talking to you on, I mean.'

'Yes, it is.' Louise caught herself grinning in the large mirror above the fireplace. She walked across and looked out of the window. She was half-expecting, *hoping* that the woman would be standing outside, waving at her. 'It is. It *is* my phone.'

'We were both in the café this morning, and—'

'Yes, I know. I've been calling,' Louise said. 'Well, my friends have.'

'Oh, I'm so sorry. This is the first time I've looked at my phone since then. Well, *your* phone, I mean. I barely use the flipping thing, if I'm honest.'

'It's fine. I'm just glad you called.'

Glad? She was bloody *ecstatic* . . .

'It just lies there most of the time and I was going to sit down and play a game. You know, that silly one with the fruit?'

'Sorry?'

'The game with the fruit. Anyway, that's when I looked at it and thought, hang on a minute, this isn't mine. Far too flashy ...'

The woman chuckled. Louise made a noise to suggest that she thought it was funny, but she was growing impatient. 'Could we meet up somewhere, swap the phones over? There are things on my phone I need quite urgently.'

'Yeah, that's the thing isn't it? People keep all sorts on their phones these days.'

'Yes.'

'Like I said, I just use it to play those daft games mostly.' The woman laughed again. 'And to phone people up, obviously.'

'So, can we?'

'Can we what?'

'Meet up,' Louise said.

'Oh, yes, of course.'

'That would be great.' In the mirror, Louise's grin was even wider. 'Thank you.'

'Well, that's why I'm calling, isn't it?' The woman made it sound obvious. 'So we can get you your phone back.'

'Yes, of course.' Louise walked back across to the window. A neighbour walked past, looked in and waved. Louise waved back. 'Are you free now? I mean, I'm free if you are. Where do you live?'

'Well—'

'I'm happy to come over and pick it up. I'm not sure how far away you are, but . . .'

'I'll be taking the dog out in about an hour,' the woman said. 'Maybe we could meet up then.'

An hour? Another bloody hour? Louise sighed, beyond caring if the woman heard it or not. 'OK. An hour's fine.'

'We usually go down to the beach. Just past the pier, you know?'

It was ten minutes' walk away. 'I'm sure I'll find you,' Louise said.

'Don't worry,' the woman said. 'You can't miss us. Scruffy thing with a black coat. That's me I'm talking about by the way, not the dog.'

'Right . . .'

The woman laughed again, hoarser this time. The noise was rattly, like maybe she was a heavy smoker. Louise was doing her best to laugh along with her, when the woman hung up.

Chapter Six

Louise

The hour crawled by, but the second it was up Louise was out of her front door and on her way towards the seafront. She hurried past the ice-cream parlour and the disused cinema she had filmed first thing that morning. She was thrilled at the thought that she would soon get the film back. She cut across the main road and on to the pier. She knew she would have the best possible view of the beach from there.

The afternoon crowd on the pier was beginning to thin out. There were still one or two people with cameras and a few fishermen hoping for some last-minute luck. Most people were heading towards the shore. There were teens looking for fun somewhere else and tired-looking parents dragging kids on a sugar high from the café at the far end. Louise found a spot between two fishermen and stared down at the stretch of beach below.

There wasn't a lot to see.

A man with a dog. Another with a kite. A couple of kids throwing stones.

It was cold. Louise was wearing boots and a knee-length Puffa jacket, but she still wasn't surprised to see a couple of swimmers. The sea looked as rough and uninviting as always, but there were always a few fanatics. A huge crowd gathered, without fail, every Boxing Day to take the plunge. It was yet another reason she loved this place so much. Characters like that. Oddballs. She thought they were entirely mad, and she would never dream of doing such a thing herself, but she was very happy that others did.

She moved a little further along to see more of the beach. A few minutes later, as her eyes tracked the movement of a black dog, she finally saw her.

What *might* be her ...

Not knowing what else to do, she waved. She was immediately embarrassed, but she kept on waving until, finally, the woman, who was several hundred yards away, looked towards her and waved back. Louise turned and walked quickly towards the sea-front. Though not quite willing to run, she made her way as fast as she could down on to the beach.

A few minutes later, the woman was waiting for her with a broad smile.

'Here you go,' she said. 'All nice and shiny.'

The woman held out Louise's phone. She was definitely older than Louise, but it was hard to work out what the age gap might actually be. She could have been anywhere between forty and sixty. Older, even. Louise sensed immediately that, however old she was, it was not something the woman gave a great deal of thought to.

Almost certainly a Boxing Day swimmer, Louise thought.

One of that sort.

There was certainly plenty of grey in the hair. It whipped around a face that was ruddy and lined. Free of make-up. She was stocky, in the shapeless black coat she had mentioned earlier. The hand that was not holding out the phone was clutched around the handles of one large plastic bag and several smaller ones. Pink nappy sacks that bulged and dangled.

Tempted to just grab it and run, Louise calmly took the phone and handed the woman's across. 'Thank you.'

'You're welcome.'

The phone sat snug and warm in Louise's hand. Like it belonged there.

'More bloody trouble than they're worth, I reckon,' the woman said.

Louise nodded, desperate to check her phone. She wanted to see what calls and messages she had almost certainly missed. She smiled awkwardly at the woman.

'My son got me this.' The woman held her own phone out towards Louise. 'So he could keep in touch, he said. Waste of time, if you ask me, except for the games. I mean, it's not like he rings me more than once a month. He lives in Leeds.'

'Does he?' Louise was barely listening.

'You been to Leeds?'

'A few years ago, I think,' Louise said.

The woman grinned, as though that were the correct answer. 'It's nice to have a bit of company, tell you the truth.' She looked at the dog that was straining at the end of its lead. 'Isn't it, boy?' She looked back to Louise. 'You walk much?'

'I run a bit. You know, to keep fit.'

'The dog keeps me fit,' the woman said. 'Out with him every day. In all sorts of bloody weather.' She looked down at the dog. 'Aren't I, you little bugger?'

'They're a lot of work, aren't they?' Louise

35

said. 'Dogs.' She watched as the woman began to wander away, muttering something to herself. She was clearly expecting Louise to follow. Louise didn't want to offend her. I mean, she'd brought her phone back, hadn't she? Not everyone would have taken the trouble. Louise snatched a last, despairing look at her phone and took a few quick steps to catch the woman up.

'You got kids?'

Louise shook her head.

'You want them?'

'Not sure.'

The woman smiled. 'Plenty of time.'

'I suppose,' Louise said. She pictured Danny suddenly in that daft beanie hat, leaning towards her screen through a cloud of vapour. It wasn't something they had talked about. Well, there didn't seem much point when they were both working so much. And when they weren't working, they wanted to be free to have fun. That was only natural, when you were young, wasn't it?

'Not everyone does, do they?' The woman nodded, serious. 'Want to get lumbered with kids, I mean.'

'Well, it's not that—'

'You think a *dog's* hard work?' She stopped

suddenly and bent to retrieve a discarded bundle of fish and chip paper. She sighed and stuffed it into her plastic bag. 'Arseholes.'

'Sorry?'

'People who drop litter. Scum of the earth. You married?'

'No.'

'Well, not everyone wants that either, and why should they? You can get married far too young. I can tell you that for nothing. End up with kids who never call and a smelly dog for company.'

Louise looked down at the dog. It was loping along at the woman's side, snout close to the shingle. 'What's his name? The dog.'

'Billy.' The woman reached down to pat the dog's head. 'He's an old boy now. Costs me a bloody fortune in vet's bills. You don't have a choice though, do you?'

'I suppose not.'

'What am I going to do, put him to sleep?'

Louise laughed, but the woman looked deadly serious.

'I mean that's how it goes, isn't it?' she said. 'I'll have to do it one day. Had to do it with plenty of dogs before this one.'

As though keen to prove there was still plenty of life left in him, the dog began barking and jumping up at the woman's legs. The woman wagged a finger and pushed him away.

'He seems lively enough,' Louise said.

'He gets excited when we walk, that's all. Rest of the time he just lies around stinking up the place. Don't you, Billy? Oh, here we go ...' The woman stopped and whipped a nappy sack from her pocket, like a magician producing a silk handkerchief. Humming to herself, she bent to scoop up a curl of dark dog shit.

Louise stared at the dog, who was panting happily. She said, 'Is that someone else's ...?'

The woman looked up at her.

'Someone else's ... mess, I mean.'

The woman nodded. 'Billy did his business back by the pier.'

'Right ...'

The woman straightened up and began tying the bag. 'Well, someone's got to pick it up, haven't they? Don't want kiddies stepping in it.'

'No. Of course not.' Just the thought of it made Louise feel a bit sick. She could smell it from where she was standing.

'Might be you stepping in it, messing up your lovely boots.'

Louise grunted. Now she felt even sicker. The boots had cost her nearly three hundred pounds.

'Selfish buggers don't clean up after their

animals, somebody else has to do the job, don't they?'

'I suppose so.' Louise had no desire to have a dog and the . . . mess had a lot to do with it. She wasn't sure she could stomach picking up her own dog's turds, let alone someone else's. 'It's very . . . public-spirited of you.'

The woman shrugged. 'I'd rub their bloody faces in it, if I could get hold of them. Honestly, I would.' She added the nappy sack to the collection dangling from her fingers and began to walk away again, whistling tunelessly.

Louise let out a quiet sigh, glanced at her watch, and followed.

Chapter Seven

Louise

'I mean, that's what happens, isn't it?' the woman said.

'What?'

'You put your whole life on a phone, so what the hell do you do when you lose it?'

'You run around like a headless chicken,' Louise said.

'That's it.'

'And moan at your boyfriend.'

The woman laughed, leaned her shoulder against Louise's.

They had been walking for half an hour, perhaps more. Now, with cliff-tops looming a mile or so ahead, they were on a stretch of beach that ran beside the golf course at the edge of the town. It was getting colder. To one side of them, tall trees bowed to the wind. On the other, the sea beat against the shingle, the light rapidly leaving it.

'Well, no harm done, that's the main thing.'

'Only because you're honest,' Louise said. 'Someone else might have tried to sell it.'

'Don't be silly.'

'I'm just saying ... it's quite an expensive one, you know?'

'Is it? I don't know anything about these things.'

Louise was suddenly embarrassed. 'Well, I mean it's a bit more expensive than others. You can pay a small fortune for a phone if you want to.'

'How much?'

'Oh, some people pay thousands. Have them covered with diamonds or whatever. You know, people with silly money.'

'I mean, how much was yours?'

'Six hundred plus,' Louise said. 'To buy it outright.'

The woman turned and stared at her. She tried to reach into her coat, struggling with the assorted bags. She moved the nappy sacks from one hand to another, finally handing one to Louise while she dug into a pocket for her phone. Louise took the bag reluctantly, held it at arm's length.

'What about this one then?' the woman asked.

Louise stared at her.

'How much would my son have paid for this one?' She held the phone up, as though Louise had never seen it before. 'My son, in Leeds.'

Louise leaned forward to look at it. She couldn't bring herself to touch it again. She knew well enough how battered and dirty it was. 'I'm not sure. It's a bit ... older. Still a few hundred, probably. Or he might have bought it second-hand.'

'A *few*?'

'Yeah, I should think.'

The woman looked horrified. She snatched back the nappy-sack and thrust the phone into her coat. 'Stupid bugger.'

'He was probably just being nice,' Louise said.

'I'd rather have had the money.'

Louise could not help but smile. Seeing it, the woman smiled too, then shook her head when Louise glanced at her watch again.

'You need to get back.'

'No, it's fine,' Louise said. 'I just wondered what the time was.'

'Don't worry.'

'It's getting a bit late, that's all.' A sudden gust of icy wind made Louise shudder.

The woman shook her head, like she was cross

with herself. She didn't look as if she was feeling the cold at all. 'Look at me. I've been rabbiting on, dragging you along and I'm sure you've got better things to do.'

'I'm meeting someone for dinner, that's all.'

'Course you are,' the woman said. 'Going anywhere nice?'

Louise couldn't make up a lie quickly enough. There were plenty of restaurants in town, but she suddenly couldn't think of one. She just said, 'I hope so.'

'Lovely,' the woman said. 'I couldn't tell you the last time I went out for dinner. Unless you count the chip shop.'

'I need to get ready,' Louise said. Nothing had been planned, but she was sure that Andrew and Stephen would be up for an evening in the pub at least.

'I am grateful, though,' the woman said. 'Honestly.' She stepped across and took Louise's hand in both of hers. The plastic bags and the dog's lead were swinging between them. 'It's a real treat to have someone to walk with. Have a good old natter to, you know?'

'Thank *you*,' Louise said.

'What for?'

'For ... well, the phone and everything.'

The woman shrugged, reddened a little.

'And I've really enjoyed ... nattering, too.' Now, Louise wasn't lying. She had been keen to get away at first, but had found herself relaxing in the woman's company. It had been nice. Or at least, it had been nicer than she'd thought it would be. Opening up to this stranger whose oddness had quickly become strangely likeable. She'd certainly never met anyone like her before.

The woman beamed and rubbed her dog's head.

Louise had only taken half a step away when the woman said, 'Why don't I drop you back?'

'Oh.' Louise shifted from one foot to the other. 'I don't want to put you to any trouble. Any *more* trouble.'

'It's no trouble, is it Billy?' The dog seemed happy enough. 'Come on, it'll be getting dark soon. It's the least I can do after dragging you a mile or more down the bloody beach. Look, my car's just there ... ' She pointed up to a track above the beach. A vehicle was outlined against a purplish sky. 'I'll have you back home in five minutes.'

Louise was hesitant. But she was also cold. 'Are you sure?'

'Positive.'

'OK, that's ... thanks.'

'Come on then.' The woman grinned and

held up the plastic bags; her collection of litter and dog shit. 'We can drop off all my treasure on the way.'

Five minutes later they had reached a rusty, mud-spattered Jeep. One of the headlights was cracked and there was a large dent in the bonnet. Once she had thrown her bags in a nearby litter bin, the woman opened the doors and led the dog towards the boot.

She nodded at Louise. 'Hop in ...'

Louise walked around and climbed into the passenger seat. She closed the door and let out a long breath. She took out her phone. Behind her she could hear the rear door open and the voice of the woman trying to coax the dog up and in.

'Come on Billy ... up you go ... good boy.'

Louise stared happily at her phone, at the familiar screensaver. As she'd expected, there were more than a dozen missed calls. From Danny, from Andrew and Stephen. She snatched happily at the few precious seconds she now had to catch up. At the chance to listen to some of the messages she could see were waiting.

She swiped and began to enter her PIN.

She froze.

The rear door slammed and a few seconds later the woman got into the car. She was huffing and puffing, the car key dangling from an enormous bunch in her fist. 'There we are, then.'

'How did you unlock my phone?' Louise asked.

The woman started the car. 'Sorry, love?'

Louise held the phone towards her. She was sweating and struggling to stop her fingers shaking. She could not believe she hadn't thought of this until now. 'It's locked, same as yours was.'

'Is it?'

'Yes. It's *locked*. You couldn't have called me on it unless you unlocked it.'

The woman was humming to herself and adjusting her mirrors. 'Oh, well, if you say so.'

'So, how did you know it?'

'How did I know what, love?'

Louise fought to stay calm. To stop herself shouting. 'My PIN?'

The woman turned in her seat and looked at her for a few seconds. Her smile was gentle, as if to a frightened child. Then with shocking speed and force, she leaned across and punched Louise in the face.

Chapter Eight

Andrew and Stephen

Andrew was watching an old black and white film when Stephen got back from the shops. They'd been shopping once already, after going to the café in the morning, but after all the drama with Louise's phone, they had forgotten a few things. Andrew would be the one doing the cooking later on, so he'd sent Stephen out to get them. Another nice bottle of wine, some posh cheese and crackers and some grapes to go with it.

There were university friends of Stephen's coming for dinner, and Andrew was keen to lay on something special. One of them was an ex-boyfriend of Stephen's, so Andrew *really* wanted to impress him.

Not that he wanted Stephen to know that.

Stephen dumped the shopping bag in the kitchen and walked through to the living room.

'Get everything?' Andrew asked.

Stephen nodded and sat down. He looked at the TV and pulled a face. Old films weren't really his thing. 'Got some expensive chocs as well. If people have coffee.'

'Lovely.'

'I thought I saw Louise.' Stephen kicked his shoes off and swung his legs across the arm of the chair.

'You *thought* you saw her?'

'Standing on the pier,' Stephen said. 'Staring out into space.'

Andrew smiled. 'Well, you saw how she was when she lost her phone. Maybe she was thinking of throwing herself off.'

'Oh, God, do you think so?'

'No, of *course* I don't.'

'Maybe I should have spoken to her.' Stephen sounded worried. 'I had all the shopping though, you know.'

'What's the problem? We only saw her a couple of hours ago.'

'I nearly did,' Stephen said. 'I nearly crossed over and went on to the pier. But the bag was heavy, and I wasn't even certain it was her. I mean, what would she be doing on the pier?'

'Maybe she's thinking of taking up fishing,' Andrew said.

Stephen laughed. He said, 'Oh, can you imagine? She couldn't even *touch* a fish. She'd be like . . . ' He waved his arms in the air. '"Oh, it's so slimy and disgusting." You know what she's like.'

Now Andrew laughed, and they sat and watched the film for a couple of minutes. Their dog came trotting in and Stephen bent to pick him up. The dog settled down quickly on his lap.

'I hope she's all right though,' he said.

Andrew was not really listening. He was still trying to watch the film. 'What?'

'Louise. I hope she's feeling a bit better.'

'Oh, course she is,' Andrew said. 'It's only a bloody phone. Nobody died.'

'I know, but like you said, she was really upset. Poor thing . . . '

They had waited while Louise went back to the café. When she had trudged back to the market a few minutes later, she was pale and shaking. She'd looked as though she might burst into tears. Like she'd just been told she had cancer or something. Andrew and Stephen had hugged her while she told them what the waitress had said. They had both agreed that the waitress was absolutely right. Whoever had taken her phone

49

was bound to bring it back. Course they would. Nobody would steal it.

It wasn't that kind of place.

Now, Andrew picked up the TV remote. He pointed it at the TV and turned the volume up. 'Don't you worry about our Louise,' he said. 'She might be a bit of a spoiled princess at times, but she's tough as old boots.'

Chapter Nine

Danny

Danny was feeling guilty.

Sitting in the pub, waiting for Sophie to arrive, he felt something like little stabbing pains in his belly. Not painful, exactly. Just annoying, like having something stuck in your teeth.

So, not *very* guilty, and not because he was meeting Sophie either. Yes, maybe some people might think that Saturday was a strange day to be talking about work. But that was what he and Sophie would be doing, at least for some of the time. That was what they'd talked about on the phone, when Sophie had called the night before. She'd remembered him saying that Louise was going to be away, she'd told him she was on her own, too. She'd wondered if they could maybe have a drink and talk about that new ad campaign for the fizzy drinks company. You know, as they were both at a loose end.

It made sense. Workmates talking about work. Nothing wrong with that, was there?

So what if it was the weekend?

So what if they were doing it in a pub . . . ?

'Yeah, love to,' Danny had said.

He was feeling guilty because he hadn't gone down to see Louise. He'd been angry when she'd asked him. I mean, so she'd lost her stupid phone. It wasn't his fault, and it wasn't that big a deal anyway, was it? She'd only wanted him to go down because she didn't want to be miserable on her own. Because she wanted a shoulder to cry on. To *moan* on. That was hardly going to be fun for him, was it? Great way to spend a Saturday, *that* would have been.

But still, sitting there and sipping his drink, he felt a bit guilty. If he'd left straight away and caught the train, he'd probably have been there by now. But it was always a hassle, and he hadn't been lying when he'd told her he had stuff to do. Nothing that was urgent, but it had needed doing. Some boring computer stuff and it was the only day he could go and buy those new shoes he wanted. He was tired anyway, plus he wanted to put his feet up later and watch *Match*

Of The Day. And he'd got this thing with Sophie, hadn't he?

This work thing.

He hadn't told Louise about *that*, obviously.

Only because there wasn't really anything to tell. The two of them were only meeting to talk about work, so why bother bringing it up?

Little stabbing pains in his belly . . .

She liked going down to the seaside place more than he did, anyway. She liked getting away and spending time on her own. She'd told him that. Yeah, he was sorry about the whole missing phone thing. It wasn't like he *wanted* her to be upset. But he knew she'd be all right. The phone was bound to turn up or get handed in, and it would be fine even if it didn't. A few glasses of wine and Louise would feel better. By the end of the day she'd be online ordering herself a new phone. Probably a few other bits and pieces to make up for the shitty day she'd had.

'Dan . . . ?'

He looked up and saw Sophie waving to him from the other side of the bar. She was wearing that tight leather jacket he liked. It looked like she'd had her hair done.

The blonde highlights.

Danny stood up and waved back. He took out his wallet so he could go and buy her a drink.

Thinking about it, he might as well buy a bottle they could share.

He watched her walk over, taking off her leather jacket.

Those little stabbing pains had gone.

Chapter Ten

Louise

Flashes of light and colour – brown and dirty-yellow – burst through the blackness like bits of a dream. She could hear sounds, too, above the buzzing in her ears. Distant and tinny one second, horribly loud the next.

A low whine, like a machine.

The happy jingle of familiar tunes.

A dog's bark.

And there was a shape. Big and blurry. *Her* shape.

There at the other end of a thin room or corridor. Swaying gently or still as a statue, as though she was watching. And each time, for those few seconds when the darkness seemed about to lift and she struggled to wake fully, Louise felt like she was about to be sick.

But it was a dream where she couldn't open her mouth ...

Stiff and dizzy, Louise grunted as her eyelids lifted. Sticky, like they'd been glued together. It was half a minute, more, until her eyes finally opened, then widened.

Bulged.

She took it all in fast, as the moan in her throat got louder. The blue washing line tied hard across her chest and arms. The peeling paint of the wooden chair she was tied to, and something tight across her mouth.

Christ ...

Tatty net curtains hung at the dirty windows, above a built-in table and U-shaped plastic seating. There was a door to the right. She guessed it was the door to *outside*. There was a smaller one to the left that she thought was probably the toilet. And there was the woman, singing along to something on a small radio. She was nodding her head. She was happily pushing and pulling at a vacuum cleaner in the tiny kitchen at the far end of the caravan.

Louise could feel something scratch against her jeans and she looked down to see the dog licking her knee. She kicked out at it and it scampered away. The woman turned to look at her. She reached down to switch off the vacuum cleaner, then leaned across to turn down the radio.

She waved, just as she had done when they met on the beach.

Louise had no idea how long ago that was.

'Sorry, did I wake you?'

Louise stared.

The woman nodded towards the radio. 'Do you like Neil Diamond? I bloody *love* Neil Diamond. I've seen him five times.'

Louise began to scream. At least she tried to, as she struggled against the washing line. The dog sighed and lay down to watch her.

The woman turned the radio off. 'I was going to wait,' she said. 'But I didn't know how long you'd be asleep for, did I? I mean, everything was such a mess, and I really wanted it to be nice for you.'

She nodded and smiled. Then she raised her arm and waved it around. 'It's not big, but you'd be amazed how much work it is to keep it clean. I don't bloody stop, some days . . .'

She picked up a cloth from the edge of the sink and began to wipe at one of the surfaces. 'Needs doing every day, more or less, and Billy doesn't help.' She wagged a finger at the dog. 'Do you, boy? Walking mud in and leaving dog hair all over everything. Can't do much about the smell,

57

I'm afraid. I've tried those plug-in things, but they're as much use as tits on a fish. I've tried all sorts, and you wouldn't believe how many cans of air-freshener we get through.'

She smiled again and shook her head. 'But doesn't matter what I do. Even if I leave the door and all the windows open. There's always something . . . doggy about the place.'

She tutted and bent to scrub hard at a stain. 'Don't worry, though. You get used to it.'

Now, Louise made even more noise. She shook her head and tried to move her legs. She struggled hard enough to tip the chair on to its back legs for a second or two.

The woman reached into the pocket of her apron and took out Louise's phone. She pressed buttons and swiped through screens. She opened apps and tapped at menus. 'Now, before I forget . . . there aren't any emails or messages that are life or death. But you're going to miss that lunch on Monday with Adam, and the meeting in the afternoon. Sorry about that. Those are the most urgent things as far as the diary goes, I think. I mean, you've got quite a lot of stuff on towards the end of the week, but we can worry about all that later.'

The woman shook her head. She puffed out her cheeks. 'I can't believe how *busy* you are. So, if you ask me, this'll be a nice change of pace for you. A bit of a break. I know you're supposed to be seeing people and all that, but if you can't make it, you can't make it. Simple as that.' She shrugged. 'I know you're not the sort of person who likes to let anyone down, but these things can't be helped, can they?'

The woman waited, like she thought Louise might answer. But Louise just stared at her, breathing heavily. She screwed her eyes shut, but only for a few seconds. When she opened them again the woman was nodding, as if that was exactly the reaction she was looking for.

'Well, I mean, these things happen, don't they? Sometimes we have to change our plans, doesn't matter how clever we think we are. How good we might be at putting these things on our phones or what have you. We *all* have plans.'

She paused and looked out of the small window into the darkness. 'But there are times when they don't work out, so we have to ... change those plans. Go with the flow. That's what my son says. Remember? The one who lives in Leeds? We just have to make the best of it and crack on. No point crying about it.'

The woman turned to Louise and smiled. She put the phone back into the pocket of her apron and went back to her wiping. 'I mean, take you and me for a start. If you've got plans and I've got ... different ones, there has to be a bit of give and take, doesn't there?' She dropped the cloth back into the sink. 'That's what friends do, don't they?' She waited, like she was expecting an answer. Then looked annoyed that she wasn't getting one. She walked slowly across to Louise and leaned down.

Louise's head dropped.

The woman wiped her hands on the front of her apron, then reached out to take hold of Louise's chin. She lifted Louise's head up. 'I *said*, that's what friends do. Isn't it?'

She stared at Louise. She didn't blink.

Louise nodded.

The woman grinned and straightened up. 'Now then,' she said. 'What shall I do us for dinner later?'

Louise shook her head.

'What about some chops?' The woman lifted a lead from the back of the door and the dog stood up. 'I'm going into town anyway, so I could easily pop to the butcher's.'

Louise bucked in her chair and shouted against the gaffer tape across her mouth.

'No? Is that a "no" to the chops?' The woman looked down at the dog and shook her head. 'Well, it's up to her, isn't it, boy? She's the one who is going to go hungry. I'm sure you'll eat them if she doesn't.'

Louise carried on shouting as the woman leaned down to put the dog's lead on.

'We won't be too long.'

The dog was already scratching at the door, keen to get out.

The woman walked across and turned the radio back on. 'There you go,' she said. 'A bit of music to keep you company.'

Louise was still shouting, and the dog started barking, and Elton John was singing about a yellow brick road, as the woman stepped out of the door and locked it behind her.

Chapter Eleven

The Woman

She parked by the supermarket and took her tartan shopping trolley out of the boot. She pushed it down to the high street. The meat would be a bit dearer in the local butcher's, but it was worth it. It would be less fatty, and she didn't want to serve fatty meat, did she? What sort of a hostess would give someone fatty meat?

That was *not* the way she treated her guests.

Louise would eat the food when she got hungry enough.

It wasn't as cold as it had been, so once she had bought the chops, she strolled to a coffee shop and sat outside with a hot chocolate. The dog lay down at her feet and went to sleep. It was dark, but the high street was still busy. She waved at a couple of people she recognised and they waved back. A man who ran one of the market stalls stopped to say hello when he walked past. He sat down and they chatted for a few minutes about this and that. The weather, the traffic, a new restaurant on the seafront.

'Supposed to be nice,' the man said.

'Don't know if it's really my thing,' the woman said.

'You should give it a try.'

'Well, it's only me, isn't it? So, what's the point? I mean, nobody wants to go to a restaurant on their own, do they?'

'Don't see why not,' the man said. 'Besides, there's plenty of places round here where you could go to meet people.'

The woman looked at him.

'You know, clubs. All sorts of groups and what have you. There's an exercise class every Sunday that my wife goes to. You know, if you fancy making some new friends.'

The woman smiled and shook her head. 'I'm fine,' she said. 'I'm very happy keeping myself to myself.'

'Just a thought,' the man said, getting up.

The woman shrugged and sipped her hot chocolate. She said, 'Thanks anyway, but I'm fine as I am. I don't go short of company.' She reached down to scratch the dog's ears. 'Do I, Billy ... ?'

The man patted the dog's head and said goodbye and, when he smiled, she smiled right back at him. She thanked him for the lovely chat. Most people round here were very friendly, she couldn't deny that. Always keen to pass the time of day. To ask how you were and pass on some local gossip. It was one of those places where everyone knew everyone else's business.

Or they thought they did.

She watched the man walk away, and she was still trying to remember his name as she took out the phone.

Louise's shiny, stupid phone.

She quickly tapped in the PIN, just as she had seen Louise do a dozen times or more. In the café. Behind her in the queue at the fishmonger's. Standing next to her at one of those market stalls . . .

It was also one of those places where it was easy to hide in plain sight.

2.6.8.2.

A bit silly to use your birthday as your PIN. I mean, that wasn't very secure, was it? Her son had told her that when he was setting up her phone. 'You can't be too careful these days, Mum,' he'd said. 'Your birthday's the first thing people will try. Think of something else . . .'

She'd used Billy's birthday instead.

Once the phone was unlocked, she opened the texts and began to write a new message.

Great news ... Got my phone back! Panic over! Feel so stupid for being so upset. What an idiot! Maybe I should keep the bloody thing handcuffed to my wrist!

She smiled, pleased with herself, and took another sip of hot chocolate. She thought for a while, then finished the message. Something funny that Louise might say.

Right, I'm catching up on emails, then wine and more wine, then sleep.

She added a couple of hearts and smiley faces, because she'd seen Louise use them. Then she signed off the way Louise always did.

Lou xoxo

She decided to send the message to Andrew and Stephen first. That hideous pair of queens Louise thought were her friends. They weren't. She'd seen that sort before and knew exactly what they were like. They were probably slagging Louise off at that very moment. Taking the piss. People like that were just vampires, she reckoned. Louise might think she'd miss them and that they'd miss her, but she was wrong. She didn't need those kind of people around her, and in the end she'd be well rid of them.

Good riddance to bad rubbish.

She pressed SEND.

The boyfriend would be next and, talk about bad rubbish, he was the worst. Love was blind, didn't they say that? Well, someone must have poked Louise's eyes out, for heaven's sake! He was good-looking, she supposed, if you liked that sort of thing. Even unshaven and in that stupid hat he was always wearing. Danny was hardly the sharpest tool in the box, though. She'd read his texts and that was pretty bloody obvious.

Worse than being thick, he wasn't *honest*.

Some of those texts and emails made it plain enough, even if poor Louise couldn't see it. The excuses. The reasons why he had to work late, why he couldn't see her. You didn't need to be clever to work it out. A few too many mentions of that girl at work. How much more obvious could it be? Thought he was being clever by mentioning her, didn't he? Thought Louise would never suspect.

Some people were too trusting for their own good.

The woman laughed out loud when that thought popped into her head. A man sitting at the next table looked at her, but she ignored him.

It wasn't hard to imagine what Danny was up to now. While the cat's away, all that. Probably having fun with that slag from the office, while Louise was ... tied up.

She laughed out loud again.

Well, he was someone else who didn't deserve Louise. One of many. She shook her head. Why did people bother with all these so-called friends, anyway? There were hundreds of names in Louise's contacts. Hundreds! She was sure that most of them didn't need to be there. People she thought were important. People she thought mattered, but whom she didn't really *know*. It was stupid.

She finished her hot chocolate. Pressed SEND.

The woman had learned a long time ago that it was better to keep people at arms' length.

It was important to choose your friends carefully.

To select them ...

She put the phone away and got to her feet. The dog heaved itself up and began sniffing at the woman's shopping trolley. She pulled him away.

'He's after my chops,' she said.

The man at the next table looked up.

'There's chops in the trolley.'

The man smiled and went back to the book he was reading.

'Don't mind me ...'

I'm just a dotty old woman with a smelly dog. Don't even give me a second thought.

I'm harmless ...

There was a busker working opposite the chemist. Some young kid with a guitar. She stopped and listened for a minute or two, then asked him if he knew any Neil Diamond songs.

The kid shook his head.

She took out her purse and tossed a pound coin into his guitar case, then walked away towards the car park.

Chapter Twelve

Louise

Louise had stopped shouting when the woman had left. There didn't seem any point and she was trying to save her strength. She struggled for a while, but the washing line was wrapped tight around her. She pushed at the tape with her tongue but it wouldn't move.

She wasn't going anywhere.

It was dark outside, but she couldn't tell how long she had been there. She didn't know how long she had been unconscious for. She had felt so dizzy when she'd woken up, so maybe the woman had drugged her somehow.

A couple of hours? More?

She felt the terror like something squirming inside her. Deep down in her guts, slick and wriggly. She had thought that people's teeth only chattered in films, but now she had to clench her jaw to stop them rattling. Same thing with her heart. She'd read books where people's hearts felt like they would 'burst out of their chest', and now she knew what that meant. It was thumping against her ribs and, however hard she tried, she couldn't slow her breathing down. It was like she was running, running, running . . .

And every question rattling around her brain made it all worse.

Why had the woman taken her?

Where was she?

Was the woman going to hurt her?

There were no answers that made any sense, and the worm in her belly just wriggled that bit harder.

But there was hope too. Just a whisper of it, beneath the screams inside her head. Someone would come, wouldn't they? She didn't know how long she had been in the woman's car, but they couldn't have gone that far, surely. It wouldn't be long before Stephen and Andrew wondered where she was. Before Danny started to get worried. Then one of them would call the police. Then the police would start looking. And the police would find her.

Wouldn't they?

Stupid thing was, she always let people know

where she was. She was sending texts all the time: *I'm at the shops, back in half an hour. Just popped into town, see you at 5.00.* Whatever. The one bloody thing her phone was really useful for, and now she couldn't do it.

Because that woman had taken it.

She began to wonder how long the woman had been planning it all. How long she had been watching and waiting. Long enough to know Louise's PIN, obviously. To know what her movements would be. To know how much she would panic when her phone went missing. How desperate she would be to get it back.

To know what an easy target she would be.

Her phone ...

She'd seen enough cop shows on TV to know that police could use a mobile phone to find people. Cell sites or whatever they were called. They could trace the signal, couldn't they? Yes, of course they could. She imagined a dot blinking on a computer screen somewhere. Her phone, calling for help. A smart detective pointing and saying, 'There she is.' Maybe Andrew or Stephen had called them and the police were already closing in.

Racing to her rescue with their lights flashing.

Until then, she just needed to keep calm. That was important. She didn't want to annoy the woman. She just needed to pretend that everything was all right. It was pretty clear that the woman wanted to be her friend. In her sick, twisted mind she thought they *were* friends. That was obvious. All that crazy stuff she was saying about wanting the place to be nice. About give and take. Louise was sure that, if she behaved and did what the woman wanted, she'd be OK. If the woman thought they were friends, she would have no reason to hurt her, would she?

Perhaps Louise could start talking to her and persuade the woman to let her go. She'd make her see sense. She'd promise the woman that she wouldn't tell anyone. She'd swear to her that she wouldn't tell a soul. Then later on she'd come back and watch as the police dragged her away. She'd be in court every day, too. *Every* day. Staring down from the public gallery and cheering when they banged the mad old bitch up.

She'd pose for photos and talk to all the reporters on the steps outside. She'd be the woman who survived. The pretty victim, smiling through tears of joy and relief.

It would be an amazing story to tell all her friends. She imagined Andrew and Stephen gasping in horror, and Danny telling her how brave she was. She'd sell her story to the newspapers, photos of her and Danny's wedding.

She'd be famous. She'd write a book, maybe. She would be *alive*.

It would soon be over, she could feel it. She closed her eyes and saw that dot again. Blinking faster, the police on their way. She imagined the woman's face as she heard the sirens getting louder. Perhaps they would burst in with guns, shoot the bitch and her stupid fucking dog ...

And suddenly that whisper of hope was cut off.

Her breathing began to race again and the worm wriggled in her belly.

She could hear a car pulling up.

Chapter Thirteen

Andrew and Stephen

Andrew and Stephen were still waiting for their guests to arrive when the messages came through. Andrew was in the kitchen and Stephen was laying the table. The alerts on their phones sounded within a few seconds of each other.

Beeping and whistling.

'Ha.' Andrew shouted through from the kitchen. 'Looks like Madam got her phone back.'

'Hang on,' Stephen said. He walked across to the CD player and turned down the classical music that was playing. 'I'm just reading it . . .'

Andrew came into the sitting room. 'So, she didn't chuck herself off the pier then.'

Stephen laughed. 'I bet she came close though.' He put his phone down and took a sip from the glass of wine he had on the go. 'Never seen

74

anyone in such a state.'

'It was *so* over the top.'

'It was bloody ridiculous.'

'And I thought *we* were supposed to be the drama queens,' Andrew said.

Stephen pulled a face. 'Speak for yourself,' he said.

'You were the one who thought she was going to kill herself.'

'I was worried,' Stephen said. 'That's all.'

'Well, now we can all relax and forget about Princess Louise for a while. So why don't you worry about laying that table instead?' Andrew walked back towards the kitchen. He shouted over his shoulder. 'You need to give those glasses a wipe.'

'Shall I give her a quick call?' Stephen said.

'What?'

Stephen picked up a glass and followed Andrew into the kitchen. 'Shall I call Louise?'

'Why?'

'I don't know ... just to say we're happy she got her phone back.'

'You saw her text,' Andrew said. 'She's probably already half-pissed by now.'

Stephen picked up a tea towel and leaned back against the work-top. He cleaned the glass and watched Andrew chop vegetables. 'What did you think of that stuff she showed us this morning? The film ... '

Andrew grunted. 'Well, it was a bit ... ordinary.'

'That's what I thought,' Stephen said. 'Didn't like to say anything, though.'

'I'm not even sure she's very good at her job.' Andrew tossed the vegetables into a saucepan. 'We can have a look at it online later, but if you ask me, she hasn't got much of an eye.'

'Except for when it comes to boyfriends,' Stephen said. 'I mean, Danny's not exactly Brain of Britain, is he, but he's nice to look at.'

Andrew turned around. 'That's how I like my men,' he said. 'Fit as fuck, but not very bright.'

Stephen threw the tea towel at him.

Chapter Fourteen

Danny

Danny heard the alert on his phone, but he had been too busy to check the text.

'Do you need to get that?'

'It's fine,' he said. 'Not important ...'

Half an hour later, when he finally looked at his phone and read Louise's message, he could feel the guilt easing a little. Those little stabbing pains that had started again an hour or so before. When he'd been following Sophie through the front door of her flat.

They'd stayed in the pub until it had started to get dark. Until they'd got through two bottles of wine. They *had* talked about work, but not for very long, and it was no more than moaning about other people in the office.

'Now, *this* is the kind of work meeting I like,' Sophie had said.

'Me too.'

'We could carry on working somewhere else if you like.'

'Sounds good.' Danny had laughed. 'I'm a workaholic, me.'

Sophie had laughed too, every bit as drunk as he was. She had reached across and laid her hand across his. 'My place is only a few stops away on the Tube.'

'That's handy.' Danny was smiling as he finished his drink.

'I've got more wine.'

'I'm not sure I could drink any more,' Danny said.

Sophie was already reaching for her leather jacket. 'Well, I'm sure we could find something else to do ...'

Now, standing and looking at the message from Louise, Danny didn't feel quite as bad as he had. He didn't feel bad at all. At least she would be happy that she'd got her phone back. It sounded as if she'd planned a nice lazy evening for herself too, which was good. So she wouldn't be sitting there worrying about him. About where he was, and what he was up to.

He tapped out a quick reply.

that's great news! call u tomorrow. D x

'Everything OK?' Sophie asked.

'Yeah,' Danny said. He hit SEND, deciding that he'd call her later on when he had some time alone. 'Just a mate.'

'Ready for a bit of overtime . . . ?'

Danny turned, grinning. He was naked, so Sophie could clearly *see* that he was. He walked back to the bed and slid in next to her.

Lying to two different women was *such* a turn-on.

Chapter Fifteen

Louise

Louise had begun to cry.

The tears fell slowly at first, then faster as they slid across the silver gaffer tape that covered her mouth. They mingled with the sweat and snot. She sucked in long breaths through her nose. The sobs were muffled and ragged against the tape, and only stopped when she heard the tones of a message alert.

Her phone.

Her eyes flicked to it straight away. She could only watch and struggle when the tone sounded again. And while the phone moved slowly across the table-top as it vibrated. She began to cry again as soon as the phone was silent. She watched and wept as the woman stepped across to pick it up and held it out for Louise to look at.

Danny (Mob): 7 Missed Calls. 1 Unread Message

'He was ringing and ringing,' the woman said. 'Earlier on. Oh, and he replied to your text.' She smiled at the confusion in Louise's eyes. 'Well, *my* text I should say. I sent him a message from you. To say you'd got your phone back.' The woman opened the text from Danny. 'Oh, look, he's pleased. That's nice, isn't it?'

Louise shook her head. The tears kept coming.

'I sent one to that gay pair as well. The ones you go to the café with. I see they haven't sent a message back.' She shook her head, disgusted. 'Can't say I'm surprised.' She stepped across and patted Louise on the arm. 'I don't think you're a very good judge of people, are you, love?' A smile appeared and became a grin. 'Well, no. *Course* you're not. You wouldn't be here if you were. I mean, you'd never have got into my car, would you? Some people are just too polite for their own good, I reckon.' She looked down at the dog, once again lying at Louise's feet. 'Aren't they, Billy?'

Louise tried to speak, but the tape held her lips together.

'What's that, love?'

Louise's moan of pain and terror was clear enough.

'Oh, I know what you're thinking. If I sent a

text, that means the police can trace your phone. Home in on it, like pigeons. They've got all that high-tech gear these days, haven't they? Well, that's all right, because I sent it from in town. When I went to fetch the chops.' She smiled. 'See? I'm not as daft as I look.'

The woman's eyes widened when the phone began to ring. A different tone. A video call coming through. 'Oh,' she said. 'Here he is again.'

She held the phone out so that Louise could see. A picture of Danny, grinning in his beanie hat.

Danny (Mob) would like FaceTime.

Louise lunged forward and the woman stepped back. She did not know that she had accidentally pressed the answer button until she heard a voice coming from the phone.

'Lou? Lou ... who's that?'

The woman looked down at the phone. Danny was peering straight at her. It looked as though he was calling from a bathroom. Quickly, the woman stabbed at the screen and ended the call.

Louise shouted, roared behind the tape.

The woman let out a long breath and shook her head. 'Honestly, I don't know what I'm doing half the time. Still, no harm done.' She reached into the pocket of her brown cardigan and produced a small, pointed thing like a paper-clip. Louise recognised it immediately. There had been one in the box when she bought her iPhone. She began to cry harder, because she knew exactly what it was for.

'Now, there's someone else that's going to have to change his plans. Your Danny, I'm talking about. Long-term, I mean.'

As she spoke, the woman pushed the tip of the pin into the side of the phone. A small tray popped out, and she expertly removed the SIM card. She nodded, like she was pleased with herself.

She said, 'There you go. That's it.'

The dog began to scratch itself.

Louise moaned behind the tape.

'I'm sure he'll be all right though. Your precious Danny. Not like it really matters. I'm not sticking my nose in or anything, but the pair of you haven't exactly been getting on lately, have you?' She held up the phone. 'All those rows about him not coming down here enough.'

She dropped the phone into her pocket and walked back to the other end of the caravan. The SIM card was still pinched between two fingers.

'All those text messages about that woman he's been working with.' She shook her head and tutted. 'You know, the blonde one in his office? It's none of my business, but I reckon he's been taking you for a ride.' She leaned back against the sink and sighed. 'If you ask me, you're well rid of him. He's clearly a bit dim, anyway. I mean, I saw that picture of her ... the blonde ... and she's not even in your league. Not even *close*.' She lowered her voice. 'And I'm no detective or anything, but what was he doing calling you from a bathroom? And why was he whispering? I mean, whose bathroom was it? You see what I'm saying ...'

The dog had begun to lick at Louise's leg again and she tried to kick him away.

'Billy, stop it!'

The woman leaned down and opened the fridge. She whistled. 'Come on, then.'

The dog trotted across as the woman pulled out a packet of ham. She told the dog to sit, then carefully removed a slice and folded the SIM card into it. The dog snatched and swallowed. After wiping her hands against her dress, the woman began bustling around. She started to sing the same Neil Diamond song to herself that had been playing on the radio when Louise had woken up.

'Do you like Neil Diamond?' she asked. 'Oh, listen to me. I've asked you that already, haven't I? Going loopy in my old age ...'

She took a large plastic bag and a few smaller

ones from a cupboard under the sink. She lifted the dog's lead, then her coat from the back of a door. The dog started to bark.

'I need to take Billy out,' she said. 'To do his business.'

Louise shook her head. She tried to say *please*.

'Don't worry, I'll get our dinner on as soon as I get back. Now, what shall I do us with these chops?' The woman fastened the lead, then started to put her coat on. 'A nice bit of mash? What about some runner beans?'

Louise began to struggle again. The chair rocked from side to side on the thin carpet as she shouted behind the tape.

The woman buttoned up her coat. 'Well, I've got some frozen peas if you don't want beans.'

Louise struggled harder. Made more noise.

Suddenly angry for the first time, the woman stepped quickly across and tore the gaffer tape from Louise's face. Louise gasped in pain. She sucked in a few fast breaths then really began to scream. The woman stepped back. She looked shocked, as if this was the very last thing she had been expecting.

She waited until Louise had stopped to take in air.

'Listen, it's up to you, love. You can be spoilt and make a silly fuss if you want, but you'll be sorry when you're starving later on. And you can scream all you like. No bugger's going to hear you—'

'Why are you doing this?' Louise asked. The words fell out of her mouth in a rush. Half gasped, half screamed.

'*Why?*' The woman looked at her, as if it was the most stupid question in the world, then moved slowly towards Louise. Her knees cracked as she knelt down in front of the chair.

Louise tried to lean away, but could not move.

The woman's face was only inches away from hers.

Her breath was bad, like an old washcloth.

'Because we all need friends, don't we?' The woman was smiling now and her voice was gentle. Almost a whisper. '*Real* friends, I mean. Not like all those names in your contact list. Friends on a phone aren't real friends, are they? Friends on Twitter and Facebook, or whatever. They're not friends who care about you. Who really *know* you. Me and you are going to be proper friends, and it's going to be lovely. Just the two of us. Because when two people really care about each other, like we do, they don't need anyone else, do they? They're happy just as they are, and that's what we'll be. Happy . . . '

Her smile was wide, showing crooked yellow

teeth and blackened gums. Her eyes were flat though, like a doll's, and Louise could do nothing but stare at herself in them.

Like that time with the seagull . . .

'So, best make sure we don't fall out,' the woman said. 'That would be just . . . terrible.'

She stood up and walked quickly to the door. She opened it for the dog and, as soon as Louise began to scream again, the woman stepped outside. She pulled a face, like the noise was hurting her ears.

'Terrible,' she said again.

She slammed the door behind her.

Chapter Sixteen

Andrew and Stephen

Andrew, Stephen and their two guests were all a little drunk. They had got through almost three bottles of wine already. There was a good deal of giggling as they gathered around the laptop Andrew had laid down on the dinner table.

As soon as the film began, Andrew began to laugh.

'What are we watching again?' said one of their guests.

'It's our friend Louise,' Stephen said. 'She films all this stuff for a fashion magazine.'

'She's your friend?'

Stephen nodded. 'Well, we don't see very much of her, but yeah.'

'So, why are you taking the piss out of her?'

Andrew was still laughing. 'We're not exactly taking the piss. I mean, she puts this stuff in a public file anyway, so she wants people to look at it.' He threw his arm around Stephen's shoulder. 'Besides, if you can't take the piss out of your friends, who *can* you take the piss out of? Look at that!' He pointed at the screen. 'I mean, it's just so badly framed . . . '

When the short film had ended, Stephen moved to shut the laptop down. Andrew quickly pushed the lid back up. He said, 'Let's have a look at some of the others.'

Stephen topped up everyone's glasses, while Andrew opened up another of the films in Louise's file. They all sat back to watch and Andrew started laughing again. He said, 'She actually wants to stop doing this stupid stuff for magazines. Says she wants to make proper films.' He pulled a face at Stephen. 'Yeah, like *that's* ever going to happen.'

A few seconds in, Stephen pointed to the screen. 'There.' He reached across and paused the playback. 'Look at that woman.'

'Which woman?' Andrew leaned closer to the screen.

'That one there, in the doorway. See her?'

Andrew stared. A woman stood in the background, in the doorway of the butcher's shop. A black dog sat at her feet. 'So?' Andrew took a drink. 'Who's she?'

'She's the same woman who was in the café this morning. The one with the dog, don't you remember?'

Andrew shrugged. 'Vaguely. So . . . ?'

'She's the one Louise thought had picked up her phone. She was in the first film as well.'

'Was she?' Andrew looked as if he'd already lost interest.

'Hang on.' Stephen opened up another video from Louise's file at random. He pressed PLAY and they watched another of the films Louise had shot around town. Half a minute into it, he pressed the pause button. 'Look, there she is again.' He pointed to the woman who was sitting on a bench reading a magazine. The same dog was lying at the end of its lead. 'In the background, same as before.'

'It's a small town,' Andrew said. 'Bound to get the same weirdos popping up every so often.'

Stephen sounded a bit less drunk suddenly. 'I just think it's a bit odd, that's all. I mean to see the same person once or twice would be OK, but she's been in three of the films now. I bet you she's in all of them.'

'You want to watch *all* of them?'

'I'm just saying. It's like she puts herself into the background of all Louise's films. Like she's watching her or something.'

One of the guests leaned across to the other. 'I told you, didn't I? Stephen *always* had an over-active imagination.'

Stephen turned to him. 'Stalkers aren't always dodgy-looking blokes, you know? There's all sorts of freaks about.'

'So, what do you suggest we do? Andrew asked.

'I don't know,' Stephen said. 'Call the police or something?'

Andrew leaned close and stared at him, serious for a few seconds until the grin appeared. 'Now, that's a call I'd like to listen in on.' He pretended to pick up a phone. 'Excuse me officer, but there's this funny old woman with a dog and she was standing in this doorway. And she was sitting on this bench. Yes, that's right, you'd better send all the men you've got.' He began laughing and rolled his eyes at their dinner guests. 'I mean, *seriously*, Stephen . . . '

'Right,' said one of the guests. 'Where's this famous pudding I've been hearing so much about?'

'Coming right up,' Andrew said. 'Now we've finished playing silly buggers.'

Stephen watched Andrew get up and hurry out to the kitchen. While the guests went back to their places at the table and poured more wine, he slowly closed the lid of the laptop.

Chapter Seventeen

Danny

Second time around, the sex had been just as good, but over with pretty quickly. Afterwards, Sophie had fallen asleep almost straight away, but Danny had stayed awake. He had waited in the dark until he was sure he could sneak into the bathroom without waking her up.

Those little stabbing pains had been stronger than ever.

He'd given it fifteen minutes or so, then crept out of bed and tiptoed to Sophie's bathroom to make the call.

He'd just wanted to say goodnight to Louise. That was all. To tell her face to face how happy he was that she'd got her phone back. To tell her he loved her, and that he was sorry he hadn't come down when she'd wanted him to. To tell her he'd call again in the morning . . .

Now, sitting naked on the edge of the bed, he wondered if he'd get back to sleep at all.

What the hell was all that about?

Who the fuck was that old woman?

He wasn't good with all that technical stuff, so maybe he was just being an idiot. I mean, if you could dial the wrong phone number, you could dial a wrong FaceTime number, right? Big, clumsy fingers. That was it. But when the call had been going through, it had said *Louise Mob* on his screen.

Hadn't it?

Maybe he'd imagined that it had.

Maybe he'd just been sleepier than he'd thought . . .

The stabbing pains were even stronger now. He held his hands across his belly. He wrapped his arms around himself.

Whoever that woman had been, she hadn't exactly looked like she fancied a chat. She looked . . . scared, if anything. Her mouth hung open and her eyes were like . . . nothing. She'd stared at him like he was the last person she wanted to see. A strange look on her face that he couldn't work out.

The room was cold. But sitting there on the

edge of the bed, that wasn't what was making Danny shiver.

Panic, that's what it was. On that woman's face. For those few seconds until she hung up, that woman . . . whoever the hell she was, looked like she was panicking.

He'd tried to call back, but hadn't been able to get through and that was when he'd heard Sophie calling him from the bedroom. Now, she was asleep again, but he'd wait until the morning this time.

Then he'd try Louise again.

Better still, if he could get away from Sophie's place quick enough, maybe he'd go straight to the station. Yeah, why not? He could jump on a train and surprise her. They could spend the day together, drive back to London in the evening.

Pretend today had never happened.

He smiled, thinking what a great idea that was. How easy it would be to put things right. But then he saw that woman's face again, and he was still shivering when he climbed back into bed next to Sophie.

Chapter Eighteen

The Woman

Twenty feet away from her front door, the grass was up around the woman's knees and she'd lost sight of her dog. She could hear him snuffling somewhere close by. Aside from the horrible noise from the caravan, there was only that and the wind moving through the trees.

The cry of a gull over the water, once in a while.

She loved this place, loved how wild it was. She loved it the most after dark, when everything was as cool and still as this. Some people would probably have called it spooky, but it was where she felt most at home.

Where she felt normal.

It was strange to think the centre of town was only fifteen minutes' drive away. No distance at all, really. Even stranger that most of the people living there didn't know places like this even existed. They didn't know much about anything, come to that. If it wasn't in a text or an email, pinging and popping up on their silly little screens.

If it wasn't there on a plate for them.

She could go there whenever she wanted, of course. She could go and have a good old look at them all. But it suited her in all sorts of ways, living somewhere so cut off. Even if it did get lonely now and again.

Just her and the dog and Neil Diamond.

Billy came running through the long grass towards her and she reached into her pocket for a chew. She fed it to him and rubbed his ears. The screams from the caravan were fading behind them.

'Not lonely any more though – eh, Billy?'

She thought about her mistake in letting Louise get near that FaceTime call, then decided she was being silly. So what if that stupid boyfriend of Louise's was worried and came looking?

So what if anybody did?

By the time they got here, there wouldn't be anything to find.

As soon as Billy had done his business and she got back to the caravan, she'd get it all over and done with.

When the dog ran away again, she moved close to the cliff's edge. Just a few feet away. She stared out over the black sea for a minute or so, then tossed the phone into the darkness. She would never see it land, of course, but that didn't bother her. Because she could imagine it. Just one more piece of black plastic stuck there at the water's edge, coming and going between the waves and the stones.

Lying next to the remains of all the others she had thrown out into the cold air. Broken and beached. Cracked glass and rusting batteries.

Like dead things washed up on the rocks.

About Quick Reads

Quick Reads are brilliant short new books written by bestselling writers. They are perfect for regular readers wanting a fast and satisfying read, but they are also ideal for adults who are discovering reading for pleasure for the first time.

Since Quick Reads was founded in 2006, over 4.5 million copies of more than a hundred titles have been sold or distributed. Quick Reads are available in paperback, in ebook and from your local library.

To find out more about Quick Reads titles, visit

www.readingagency.org.uk/quickreads

Quick Reads is part of The Reading Agency,
the leading charity inspiring people of all ages and all backgrounds to read for pleasure and empowerment. Working with our partners, our aim is to make reading accessible to everyone.
The Reading Agency is funded by the Arts Council.

www.readingagency.org.uk Tweet us @readingagency

The Reading Agency Ltd • Registered number: 3904882 (England & Wales) Registered charity number: 1085443 (England & Wales) Registered Office: Free Word Centre, 60 Farringdon Road, London, EC1R 3GA The Reading Agency is supported using public funding by Arts Council England.

We would like to thank all our funders and a range of private donors who believe in the value of our work.

LOTTERY FUNDED

THE
READING
AGENCY

Quick Reads has something for everyone

Stories to make you laugh

DEAD MAN Talking
RODDY DOYLE

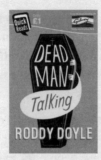

Two women, one man...
RED FOR REVENGE
Fanny Blake

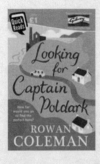

Looking for Captain Poldark
ROWAN COLEMAN

JOJO MOYES
Paris for ~~Two~~ One

A BABY AT THE BEACH CAFÉ
Lucy Diamond

EDITED BY VERONICA HENRY
ANNIVERSARY
Ten tempting stories from ten bestselling authors

Stories to make you feel good

Stories to take you to another place

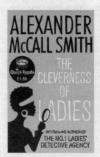

ALEXANDER McCALL SMITH
THE CLEVERNESS OF LADIES
BESTSELLING AUTHOR OF THE NO.1 LADIES' DETECTIVE AGENCY

Jenny COLGAN
a Very Distant Shore

Stories about real life

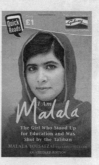

Stories to take you to another time

Stories to make you turn the pages

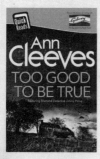

For a complete list of titles visit

www.readingagency.org.uk/quickreads

Available in paperback, ebook and from your local library

Why not start a reading group?

If you have enjoyed this book, why not share your next Quick Read with friends, colleagues, or neighbours?

The Reading Agency also runs **Reading Groups for Everyone** which helps you discover and share new books. Find a reading group near you, or register a group you already belong to and get free books and offers from publishers at **readinggroups.org**

There is a free toolkit with lots of ideas to help you run a Quick Reads reading group at **www.readingagency.org.uk/quickreads**

Share your experiences of your group on Twitter

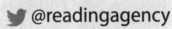 @readingagency

Continuing your reading journey

As well as Quick Reads, The Reading Agency runs lots of programmes to help keep you and your family reading.

Reading Ahead invites you to pick six reads and record your reading in a diary to get a certificate **readingahead.org.uk**

World Book Night is an annual celebration of reading and books on 23 April **worldbooknight.org**

Chatterbooks children's reading groups and the **Summer Reading Challenge** inspire children to read more and share the books they love **readingagency.org.uk/children**

THE DI TOM THORNE SERIES
WHERE IT ALL BEGAN

The first DI Tom Thorne thriller

Alison Willetts has survived a stroke, deliberately induced. In leaving Alison Willetts alive, the police believe the killer's made his first mistake. Then DI Tom Thorne discovers the horrifying truth: it isn't Alison who is the mistake, it's the three women already dead.

Thorne must find a killer whose agenda is disturbingly unique, and the one person who holds the key to the killer's identity is unable to say anything . . .

The gripping follow-up to *Sleepyhead*

One woman is followed home on the tube and strangled to death in front of her child. At the same time, a second body is discovered at the back of King's Cross Station. And these grisly events echo the murder of two other women, months before.

DI Tom Thorne comes to a horrifying conclusion. This can't be the work of just one serial killer.

And two are more deadly than one . . .

THE DI TOM THORNE SERIES

CATCH UP WITH THE LATEST CASES

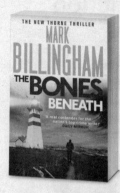

'Confirms Thorne as a memorable flawed hero' *Daily Mail*

Stuart Nicklin, the most dangerous psychopath DI Tom Thorne has ever put behind bars, promises to reveal the whereabouts of a body he buried twenty-five years before.

But only if Thorne agrees to escort him.

When new bodies are added to old, Thorne faces the toughest decision he has ever had to make . . .

'Ingenious' *The Guardian*

Two schoolgirls are abducted in a small market town, driving a knife into the local community where Tom Thorne's partner, Helen Weeks, grew up. A place full of secrets and dangerous lies.

When police believe they have the culprit in custody, Thorne finds himself on a collision course with the locals, and a merciless killer . . .